# FIRE ENGINES

**Please visit our web site at: www.garethstevens.com**
**For a free color catalog describing Gareth Stevens Publishing's**
**list of high-quality books and multimedia programs,**
**call 1-800-542-2595 or fax your request to (414) 332-3567.**

Library of Congress Cataloging-in-Publication Data available upon request from publisher.
Fax (414) 336-0157 for the attention of the Publishing Records Department.

ISBN 0-8368-3045-8

First published in 2002 by
**Gareth Stevens Publishing**
A World Almanac Education Group Company
330 West Olive Street, Suite 100
Milwaukee, WI 53212 USA

Text and photos: Eric Ethan, except photo on p. 13 © Eric Anderson/Visuals Unlimited
Cover design and page layout: Tammy Gruenewald

Printed in the United States of America

1 2 3 4 5 6 7 8 9 06 05 04 03 02

by Eric Ethan

**Gareth Stevens Publishing**
A WORLD ALMANAC EDUCATION GROUP COMPANY

This fire engine is ready to leave the station. Fire engines carry the equipment needed to fight fires and to rescue people who need help.

R0401347386

A fire engine has hoses and ladders on it. The ladders are very tall so firefighters can reach high places.

Some equipment on fire engines helps save lives. This firefighter is holding a piece of equipment called the jaws-of-life. It is used to cut through metal.

Firefighters wear special clothing. This clothing protects them from heat and smoke. A mask helps them breathe.

The water a fire engine uses usually comes from a fire hydrant. A hose connects the fire hydrant to the fire engine, and the water is pumped through this hose.

If there is not a fire hydrant nearby, a special truck fills a canvas pool with water. Water is pumped to the fire engine from the canvas pool.

Firefighters can now use this water to put out a fire. They use hoses on the fire engine to spray the water.

Special instruments on the fire engine control the amount of water that goes through the hoses.

These firefighters are practicing so they will be ready for a real fire emergency.

# GLOSSARY

**canvas** (KAN-vas): strong cloth.

**control** (kun-TROLL): have power over.

**equipment** (ee-KWIP-ment): the tools a person uses to do a job.

**fire hydrant** (FIRE hi-drant): a large pipe through which firefighters get water to put out fires.

**practicing** (PRAK-tiss-ing): getting better at something by doing it over and over.

**rescue** (RESS-keyu): to save someone from harm.

# MORE BOOKS TO READ

*Drive a Fire Engine.* Mary Atkinson
(DK Publishing)

*Fire Truck Nuts and Bolts.* Jerry Boucher
(First Avenue Editions)

*Tonka Fire Truck to the Rescue.*
Ann Matthews Martin (Scholastic)

# WEB SITES

Fire Truck Home Page
*www.nfpa.org/sparky/firetruck/index.htm*

Kern County Fire Department
*www.co.kern.ca.us/fire/media/index.htm*

# INDEX